SPLASH LANDING

Jan Burchett and Sara Vogler

Illustrated by Alex Paterson

Orion
Children's Books

First published in Great Britain in 2014
by Orion Children's Books
a division of the Orion Publishing Group Ltd
Orion House
5 Upper St Martin's Lane
London WC2H 9EA
An Hachette UK company

1 3 5 7 9 10 8 6 4 2

The Orion Publishing Group's policy is to use papers that are natural, renewable and recyclable products and made from wood grown in sustainable forests. The logging and manufacturing processes are expected to conform to the environmental regulations of the country of origin.

A catalogue record for this book is available from the British Library.

ISBN 978 1 4440 1180 7

Printed in Great Britain by Clays Ltd, St Ives plc

www.orionbooks.co.uk

For Jayden Leo Zachary Dyche

J.B. & S.V.

For Finlay

A.P.

CONTENTS

Tom's New Pet

Whoosh!

Tom Bright woke up with a start. What was that?

Wheeeeeeee!

He heard something shoot past his bedroom window.

Sper-lash!

It had landed in the garden pond.

Glug. Glug. Glug.

It was sinking.

Was it a frog?

Was it next door's cat diving off the roof?

Or could it be a flying crocodile?

If there was a flying crocodile in his pond, Tom wanted to know what it was doing there. Especially at six o'clock in the morning. He raced down to the back garden. The water was bubbling like a witch's cauldron.

Tom watched as a strange creature bobbed to the surface. It certainly wasn't a flying crocodile. It was a lot smaller, for a start. And it was purple with yellow spots.

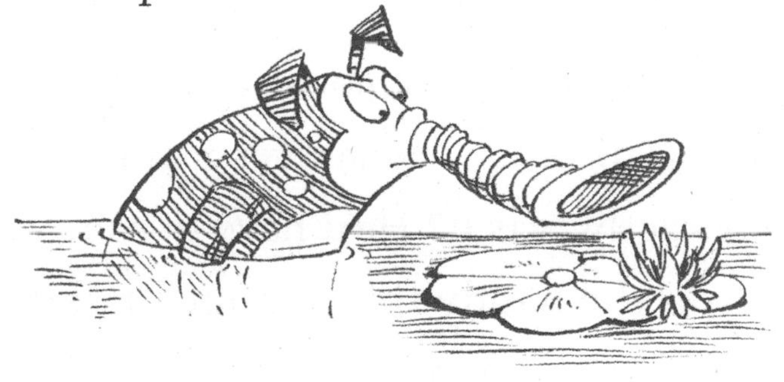

It stuck out its long trumpet nose and sniffed a lily pad.

Then it paddled over and sniffed the bank.

Now it was sniffing Tom's foot. It looked up at him and its eyes swivelled in horror.

"Zoops!" it exclaimed and splashed off to hide in the reeds. "You haven't seen me," came its gruff voice. "Go away."

It was a talking animal! Tom was delighted. He'd never met a talking animal before – well, apart from the giraffe at the zoo that had said hello to him once.

Now, Tom had discovered a new sort of creature. He'd be famous! Tom and his amazing talking . . . whatever it was. But what exactly was it? He'd have to ask. That was the handy thing about a talking animal. You could talk to it.

He bent down to coax the strange thing out of its hiding place.

Hello?

"Haven't you gone yet?" it asked, its round eyes appearing between the reeds.

"No, I'm still here," called Tom. "But it's all right. I'm ever so friendly. You don't have to hide."

"Yes, I do," the creature called back. "I'm on a secret mission. I'm not meant to be seen."

Secret mission? thought Tom. *This is sounding better and better!* "I've already seen you," he said. "You might as well come out."

The creature paddled back into view, its spotty arms and legs flapping wildly. It scrambled onto the bank and plonked itself down next to Tom. It had a big round tummy and two flat feet.

"What's your name?" asked Tom.

"I'm Fizz," it said, squeezing the water out of its nose. "What's yours?"

"I'm Tom," said Tom. "I live here. Where do you come from?"

"A long way away," said Fizz, mysteriously.

"The North Pole?" asked Tom.

"Further than that," said Fizz.

"The moon?" asked Tom.

"Don't be silly," said Fizz. "Nothing lives on the moon."

"Where, then?" demanded Tom.

"Saturn," said Fizz.

"Cosmic!" exclaimed Tom. He knew all about Saturn. The planet had rings round it and was squillions of miles away. Fizz was an alien from outer space!

"I'm a Satnik from Saturn," Fizz went on. "Satniks love nothing better than going on secret missions to explore other planets. *My* secret mission is to find out about Earth and make a report."

"Where's your spaceship?" asked Tom. He looked up and down the garden, hoping to see a flying saucer with flashing lights and lots of smoke.

"It crashed in there," said Fizz, pointing to the pond.

"A spaceship wouldn't fit in there," gasped Tom.

"It shrank, of course," said Fizz. "I'm normal size again now I've popped out."

"Will the spaceship be all right?" asked Tom, looking doubtfully at the murky water. He remembered dropping his lunch box in there once. By the time Dad had fished it out, it was green and full of tadpoles.

"Of course it will," said Fizz cheerfully. "No one can see it. Now I am going to disguise myself as an Earth animal. Then no one will know I'm a Satnik – except for you. I will pretend to be a dog. Watch this!" He bent down and began to eat the grass. "Moo!" he said with his mouth full.

"That's a cow," said Tom, trying not to laugh.

"It's a dog," insisted Fizz. "I'll show you."

He twisted his ear.

Ping!

A silver cube shot out, transformed itself into a tiny computer and landed on his hand.

"This is my Satpad," Fizz explained. "My Satpad knows a few things about Earth already."

He poked the keys with his nose and showed Tom the screen. "See?"

"The picture's too small for me," said Tom.

"Sorry," said Fizz, tapping some more keys. The image of a large cow shimmered in the air in front of Tom.

"That's definitely a cow," said Tom.

"Not a dog?" asked Fizz.

"No," replied Tom.

"What a relief," said Fizz. "That green stuff tasted horrible." He poked the keys again and looked at the screen. "Aha! I've got it now."

He scuttled up the shed wall and began to spin a web. "*Now* I'm a dog," he said.

"No, you're not," said Tom. "You're a spider."

"What a relief," said Fizz, jumping down. "I didn't have enough legs."

"There must be something wrong with your Satpad," said Tom.

The Satpad folded itself into a cube and flew back into Fizz's ear. "I expect it got damaged when the ship nearly hit Mars," Fizz said. "Its sprungles have been flobbered."

"What do you mean?" asked Tom.

"It's got its animals in a muddle," explained Fizz. He looked up at Tom, his eyes swivelling in his purple head. "How am I going to find out about being a dog?"

"Don't worry," said Tom. "I've got a kind of Satpad too – it's called a computer. It'll show you how to be a dog. Follow me, but you must be quiet."

"No problem," said Fizz, his big feet stomping along loudly behind Tom.

"Like this," said Tom, tiptoeing up the stairs. Fizz tiptoed after him.

Tom showed Fizz the laptop in his bedroom.

"That's big," said Fizz. "How does it fit in your ear?"

"It doesn't," said Tom. "But it's very useful. Look." A video of a dog appeared

on the screen. The dog scampered about, barked, dug holes in a vegetable patch and chewed up a slipper. Then a lot of people chased after it, looking cross.

"Zoops!" said Fizz happily. "What fun!"

"Wrong dog," said Tom. "I need to find one that's well-behaved."

But it was too late. Fizz ran around Tom's bedroom on all fours, skidded to a halt and began to dig up the carpet. "It's easy being a dog. Moo!"

"Woof, you mean," said Tom.

"Woof," agreed Fizz, shaking Tom's pillow in his teeth.

"Are you going to live in my pond while you're here?" asked Tom. "Only, dogs don't usually live in ponds."

Fizz twisted his ear.

Ping!

His Satpad popped out again. A big list wobbled in the air.

"Well, at least this is working properly," said Fizz, reading the list. "My next job is to make a dog nest."

"Dogs don't have nests," Tom told him.

"Don't they?" said Fizz. "Where do they live, then?"

Fizz's Important List

By Fizz.

1. Do not go near Mars.

2. Do not land in water.

3. Do not let Earthlings know you're an alien.

4. Pretend to be a dog.

5. Make a dog nest.

6. Explore Earth.

"They live with their families," said Tom. "They're pets."

"But I don't know any Earth families," said Fizz sadly.

"You know me," said Tom. A great idea suddenly jumped into his brain. "You can live here with me and my family while you're on your mission. Would you like that?"

"Yes, please," said Fizz, cheering up at once.

"You'll just have to keep pretending to be a dog whenever anyone else is around," said Tom. "And don't forget – dogs can't talk. They just say woof."

"Woof!" said Fizz, rolling over onto his back and panting.

"I can't wait to tell Zack," said Tom. "He's my best friend."

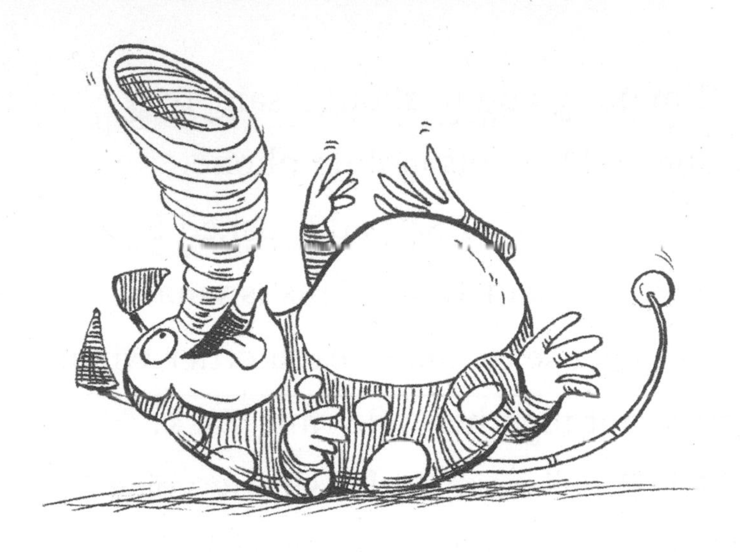

"Will he keep my secret?" asked Fizz.

"Definitely," said Tom. "That's what best friends do."

"That's OK, then," said Fizz. "Does Zack live here?"

"His house is right at the other end of the street," said Tom. "I'll call him straight away."

Fizz looked amazed. "You must have a loud voice!" he exclaimed.

"I'm not going to shout," said Tom. He showed Fizz his mobile phone.

"Is that another Satpad?" asked Fizz.

"Sort of," said Tom. "This is what Earthlings use to talk to each other when they're not together." He rang Zack.

"Hi, Tom," came Zack's sleepy voice. "What's going on? It's really early."

"I've got an incredible surprise for you," said Tom.

"Moo," Fizz put in.

"Are you on a farm?" asked Zack.

"Course not," said Tom. "I'm in my bedroom."

Zack gasped. "Why is there a cow in your bedroom?"

"There isn't a cow in my bedroom," Tom told him. "Get here as soon as you can and you'll find out the surprise."

"Moo!" added Fizz. "I mean, woof."

Tom heard his dad clattering about in the kitchen. "It's time for breakfast," he told Fizz as he pulled on his clothes. "I'll bring you up some food. What do you eat?"

Fizz rubbed his tummy. "Have you got any Splotnurbs?" he asked.

"We don't have Splotnurbs on Earth," said Tom.

"Then I'll have Dicklebubs," said Fizz.

"We don't have those either," said Tom. "How about Wheaty Krisps?"

"Yes, please," said Fizz. "They sound delicious."

Tom sneaked a large bowl of cereal up to his bedroom and they began to eat.

"These are even better than Splotnurbs," said Fizz, munching away.

The doorbell rang. "That'll be Zack," Tom told Fizz. "You practise being a dog and I'll bring him up."

He bounded down and flung the front door open. Zack stood there, an eager smile on his face.

"I got here as quickly as I could," he said. "What's the surprise?"

"Shhhh!" hissed Tom, looking round in case his mum or dad had heard. "It's upstairs – and it's top secret!"

They dashed up to Tom's bedroom.

Fizz was sitting on the bed, chewing a slipper.

Zack's mouth dropped open. "Wow!" he gasped. "What's that?"

"This is Fizz," said Tom. "He's a Satnik. He comes from Saturn."

"Hello, Zack!" said Fizz.

"Er . . . hello, Fizz," said Zack in astonishment.

Tom told Zack the whole story while Fizz pulled everything out of the wardrobe. ". . . and he's going to stay here and pretend to be my dog," Tom finished.

"But he doesn't look like a dog," whispered Zack.

"Moo," said Fizz.

"And he doesn't sound like a dog," added Zack.

"He'll be fine," said Tom. "We'll just have to train him up. Then we'll tell Mum and Dad that he's a rare breed of dog that needs a home. They won't mind." He looked out of the window. Dad was mowing the lawn.

"I'm off to the shops!" Mum called

up the stairs. "Back soon." They heard the door shut and a car drive away.

"Quick!" said Tom, fetching a ball from under his bed. "We'll start the training in the front garden."

As soon as they got down into the garden, Tom threw the ball across the grass.

"Fetch, Fizz!" he called.

Fizz looked at him. "But you've just thrown it away," he said, puzzled. "Why do you want me to get it back?"

"Because that's what dogs do," said Tom.

"Dogs must be stupid," said Fizz. He picked up the ball and threw it back.

"Your mum and dad will never believe he's a dog at this rate!" groaned Zack.

"They will," said Tom, confidently. "We just have to get Fizz to be a bit more dog-like."

Tom had finally managed to teach Fizz to pick up the ball in his mouth like a proper dog when they heard the sound of a car. It was Mum. She was back from shopping and she had seen Fizz!

"What is that?" she demanded.

"This is Fizz, Mum," said Tom. "He's a dog."

Mum stared at Fizz. "He doesn't look like a dog," she said.

"Moo!" said Fizz.

"And he doesn't sound like a dog," said Mum.

"You're meant to go woof," whispered Zack.

"Woof!" said Fizz.

"He's a rare breed," said Tom quickly. "He's a long-nosed . . . er . . ."

". . . satapoodle?" put in Zack.

"He's a funny colour," said Mum.

"Satapoodles are always like that," said Tom.

"And he's ever so well-behaved," added Zack.

Fizz began to run round the front garden. He bounced off the gate, somersaulted over the car and jumped up and down in the flowerbeds.

"Stop that!" yelled Mum. "Bad dog!" She set off after him, waving her arms. Fizz ran even faster.

"Zoops!" he called as he raced past Tom. "This is great. She thinks I'm a dog. We're playing chase!"

At last, Tom's mum cornered Fizz.

Fizz jumped up at her, knocking her into a hedge.

Tom and Zack pulled her out.

"Who does he belong to?" asked Mum crossly as she picked twigs out of her hair.

"Us," said Tom. "He needs a home so he's come to live with us."

"Woof," said Fizz, nodding. He trotted off and began to dig up a pansy.

"He can't stay here," said Mum. "We'll take him to the animal rescue centre. I'll drive him there now."

"But you mustn't!" exclaimed Tom. "He's got to stay."

"He'll be no trouble," added Zack.

Fizz pulled up the pansy and dropped it at Mum's feet. Then he scampered away to attack the shopping.

"He's going to the rescue centre," said Mum, rescuing the fish fingers, "and that's final." She rummaged in her bag. "How odd, I had my keys a minute ago. Where are they?"

She began to search her pockets.

"What are we going to do?" Tom whispered to Zack.

"We have to show her that Fizz would be a great pet," said Zack.

Tom prowled round the garden, thinking. "I've got it!" he said at last. "If Fizz bravely saved Mum's life from an avalanche, I bet I'd be allowed to keep him."

"We'd have to find an avalanche first," Zack reminded him.

"Or pulled her out of a raging river?"

Zack shook his head. "No raging rivers near here."

"Well, there must be something he could do . . ." Tom scratched his head.

Zack suddenly elbowed him in the ribs. "Look at Fizz!" he whispered. "He's helping your mum find her keys. We must stop him."

"Here, Fizz!" called Tom. "Sit!"

Fizz bounded up on all fours. "Sorry, I'm busy," he panted. "I'm playing fetch with your mother. She's thrown away something called 'keys' and now she wants them back."

"But she mustn't find them," said Zack urgently.

Fizz wasn't listening. He twisted his ear.

Ping!

Out popped his Satpad. Mum was

poking about under the car. Fizz pointed his Satpad at her. An image of car keys shimmered in the air.

Bleep . . . bleep . . . bleep, went the Satpad.

"My Satpad has a super Satpower," said Fizz happily. "It finds things. I just follow the bleeps."

He trotted off towards the house. The boys ran after him. The bleeps were getting louder.

"Stop him!" shouted Zack.

Tom made a dive for Fizz but Fizz was going too fast.

Bleep, bleep, bleep.

Fizz skidded to a halt by the drain. He stuck his nose down it.

"Zoops!" he cried triumphantly as he pulled his nose out again. "I mean, woof!"

"No," groaned Tom. Mum's car keys hung from the end of Fizz's nose.

"Quick, hide them!" whispered Zack.

But Mum had seen the keys. She ran over and took them from Fizz. Tom was horrified. They'd be off to the rescue centre now. He could just imagine what would happen when they turned up with Fizz.

But to his astonishment, Mum bent down and hugged Fizz!

"Clever dog," she said. "What a good boy!"

"Woof," said Fizz happily as she tickled him under his chin.

"I'm not taking you to the rescue centre," Mum went on. "You're going to be our pet, Fizz. You're going to live with us. Would you like that?"

"Moo!" said Fizz, wagging his whole body.

"Funny dog," laughed Mum, patting his head.

"What's this?" came a voice. It was Dad with his mower.

"This is Fizz," said Mum. "He's a satapoodle and we've adopted him."

"I've always wanted a dog," said Dad. "He's a funny colour, though."

"Satapoodles are always like that," said Mum.

"Rightio," said Dad. He began to mow the front lawn.

"I knew they wouldn't mind," said Tom, as they took Fizz round the back.

"And being a dog is easy," said Fizz. He ran to the pond and perched on the side, ready to dive in.

"What are you doing?" asked Tom.

"I'm going to tell the others," explained Fizz.

"Others?" asked Zack.

"Of course," declared Fizz. "There are a lot of things to explore on your planet. I couldn't do it all on my own."

"So there are more Satniks in my pond?" gasped Tom.

"That's right," said Fizz cheerfully.

"*Cosmic!*" shouted Tom and Zack together.

REPORT

NAME

Fizz

EARTH IDENTITY

satapoodle

REPORT

Earthlings are very friendly but their Satpads are too big to fit in their ears.

They are also very strange.

They throw things away and then they want them back.

Earthlings have pet dogs. The pet dogs have to fetch the things the Earthlings throw away. Then the Earthlings throw them away again!

And then they say, 'Fetch!'

Top Tricks

Tom was dreaming. Crowds of spotty little aliens were popping out of his pond. They were poking him and mooing in his ear.

He opened his eyes.

Fizz was poking him with his nose.

"Moo!" he said in his ear. "I mean, woof. Come on. We'll be late!"

Tom jumped out of bed. "Am I going to meet your Satnik friends this morning?" he asked eagerly.

"There's no time for that!" said Fizz. "Your mum's been calling you. She says you'll be late for school. I don't know what school is so I'm going to investigate it."

"Cosmic!" exclaimed Tom. School would be incredible with Fizz there – even better than the time the caretaker's tarantula escaped and crawled up the head teacher's trouser leg.

Tom was dressed and ready in five minutes. He was just taking Fizz down the path to meet Zack when Mum called him back.

"Where are you going with Fizz?" she asked.

"To school," said Tom.

"You can't take a dog to school!" Mum told him.

"But he'll be ever so good," Tom begged.

"Dogs don't go to school," said Mum firmly. "He's staying here."

"Sorry, Fizz," Tom whispered. "I'll see you when I get home."

"Don't worry," Fizz whispered back. "I'll find another way to investigate school."

"Remember, you're a dog," Tom reminded him. "Don't moo at Mum!"

"Woof!" said Fizz.

Tom and Zack called for Daisy. They didn't like walking to school with Daisy and Daisy didn't like walking to school with them, but their mums said they had to.

Daisy marched ahead in her wellies. She always wore wellies – green wellies with flowers on. Daisy's dad worked at the local wildlife park and she helped him muck out the elephants every morning before school.

Tom suddenly stopped dead.

"What's the matter?" asked Zack.

"Something's just jumped into my hood," whispered Tom. "I bet it's Fizz. He wanted to investigate school but Mum said he had to stay at home."

"This'll be brilliant!" said Zack. "As long as we keep him out of sight."

"What are you two whispering about?" demanded Daisy, whipping round.

"Superheroes," said Zack.

"Football," said Tom at the same time.

"Superheroes playing football," said Zack.

"It didn't sound like that to me," said Daisy, and she eyed them suspiciously the rest of the way to school.

When they reached their cloakroom Tom pretended his coat zip was stuck. Zack pretended to help him. They waited for Daisy to go through the door into the classroom.

But Daisy wasn't in a hurry. She slowly hung up her coat and slowly took her wellies off. She slowly changed into her plimsolls. At last she walked slowly into

the classroom, giving them one more suspicious look.

Zack pulled open Tom's hood.

"There's nothing there," he said.

"I must have been imagining things,"

sighed Tom, as they went to take their seats.

Miss Keane, their teacher, was happily arranging a bunch of begonias in a vase. "Welcome, class," she trilled. "Hope you're ready for lots of hard work. Remember my motto – *Fun, fun, fun for everyone!*"

"It would have been more fun if Fizz had come to school," Tom muttered to Zack.

Zack nodded. "Hard work doesn't sound like fun to me."

Daisy jumped to her feet, knocking her chair over with a clatter. "Tom's coat is dancing round the cloakroom!" she gasped.

Everybody looked. It was true!

Tom's coat was doing a jig in the air and its empty sleeves were waving at them.

"Fizz must be here after all," whispered Tom eagerly.

"How's he doing that?" Zack whispered back.

"I don't know," said Tom, "but it's cosmic!"

"This is most exciting," said Miss Keane. "I'll go and see what's happening."

"We've got to stop her!" hissed Zack. "She'll see Fizz."

The boys launched themselves at the door.

"We'll go," said Tom, blocking her way.

"It's probably just the wind," added Zack.

They darted into the cloakroom and shut the door behind them.

The coat was now skipping across the floor. A jacket hopped off its peg and did a somersault and three backpacks bounced along the bench. Then they all fell in a heap in front of the boys.

Tom and Zack heard a chuckle from somewhere near the floor. They bent down and peered under the bench.

A strange little creature peered back at them. It had big round eyes, black and white striped fur and corkscrew ears. It was holding a Satpad in its pointy claws.

"Good morning to you, Tom and Zack!" it said in a jolly voice. "I'm Toppo. I'm Fizz's friend. Thanks for the lift to school, Tom."

"So it was *you* in my hood!" cried Tom.

"Of course," said Toppo, bouncing out. "Did you like my Top Toppo Trick? I did it with my Satpad. It has a super Satpower. It makes things fly. Look." He waved it at the pile on the floor. The coats and bags flew back to their pegs.

"That's amazing!" said Tom.

"I thought you'd enjoy it," replied Toppo. "There's nothing I like better than playing tricks, but now I must start investigating school."

"You can't do that!" said Zack.

Toppo's whiskers twitched and he began to laugh. "Don't be silly," he said. "Fizz told me I must come and investigate instead of him. He said that dogs can't come to school. So I'm not going to pretend to be a dog."

He tapped the keys of his Satpad with one claw. "Fizz made me a list so I know what to do." The list wobbled in the air. "Fizz is good at lists," he told them.

"I'm up to number four," Toppo went on proudly. "I'm going to disguise myself

as an Earth rabbit. I'll zip about and make honey and no one will suspect I'm an alien." He waved his Satpad over his head and flew round the cloakroom, buzzing.

"That's not a rabbit," said Tom. "That's a bee."

Toppo grinned. "You're wrong there," he said. He used his Satpad to beam a picture in front of their noses.

"That's definitely a bee," said Zack.

"Rabbits don't go buzz," explained Tom.

"And they can't fly," said Zack.

"And they certainly don't make honey," added Tom.

"Zoops!" said Toppo. He checked his Satpad again. "I've got it now." He tucked his legs underneath him and slithered round the cloakroom, hissing loudly.

"That's a snake!" laughed Zack.

"Does a snake look like a rabbit?" asked Toppo hopefully.

"Not enough legs," said Tom.

"And too much tail," put in Zack.

Toppo's Satpad folded up and popped into his ear. "I think its sprungles have got flobbered," Toppo sighed.

"Sprungles . . . flobbered?" Zack repeated.

"He means his Satpad's got its animals in a muddle," explained Tom.

"It must have got damaged when our spaceship nearly hit Mars," said Toppo.

"Don't worry," Zack told him. "We'll show you what rabbits do."

He hopped up and down the cloakroom. Tom joined in.

"What are you doing?" Daisy was standing in the doorway. Tom and Zack stopped hopping. Toppo zipped behind a lunchbox.

"We're doing our exercises," said Tom.

"We're keeping our ears warm," said Zack at the same time.

"We're exercising our ears!" said Tom.

Daisy gave them one of her suspicious looks. "Miss Keane says you have to stop making silly noises and come back in," she told them. She disappeared into the classroom.

Two corkscrew ears appeared from behind the lunchbox.

"I know all about being a rabbit now," said Toppo cheerfully. "I'll go and investigate school straight away."

"No," said Zack.

"Why not?" asked Toppo.

"Dogs aren't the only ones not allowed at school. Rabbits aren't, either," explained Zack.

"Stay here," said Tom. "We'll come back at playtime for you. We'll help you investigate then."

"But it must be secret," added Zack.

"That sounds like a good plan," agreed Toppo. "I'll practise being a rabbit while I wait. Buzz!"

"Rabbits don't buzz!" Tom reminded him.

"In fact, rabbits don't say much at all," said Zack.

"I won't forget," said Toppo, cheerfully.

Miss Keane was writing on the whiteboard as the boys took their seats.

"You've got some catching up to do!" she called over her shoulder. "Forty fabulous spellings to copy down."

They had just got to the twenty-ninth spelling when the books in the library corner began to jiggle.

"Toppo's playing another trick," Tom whispered to Zack. "Cosmic!"

"That's great," Zack whispered back, "as long as he stays hidden."

A dirty paintbrush floated up to the ceiling. It painted a green smiley face and then floated back down.

Some of the class were nudging each other and pointing.

"Look!"

"Did you see that?"

"It must be magic!"

The vase of flowers on Miss Keane's desk slowly rose into the air.

The vase hovered above Miss Keane.

The class gasped.

The vase began to tip . . .

Tom jumped up, leapt onto the teacher's desk and grabbed it. A damp begonia plopped onto Miss Keane's head.

"Goodness gracious!" exclaimed their teacher, snatching the vase from him. "What are you doing, Tom?"

"It was the wind again," explained Tom.

"It was like a hurricane, Miss. It blew that vase right into the air!"

"Tom saved you from a soaking," called Zack.

The class clapped.

Tom bowed and went back to his seat.

"Thank you, Tom," said Miss Keane. "How interesting! We've never had a hurricane in the classroom before!"

"What's going on?" hissed Daisy across the table.

"Nothing," said Tom, looking innocent.

Daisy didn't seem convinced.

"We need to be alert," Zack whispered in Tom's ear. "Toppo could do anything with that Satpad! You nearly got into trouble."

"Let's hope he stays safely hidden in the coats," said Tom.

The classroom door swung open. A green wellington boot with flowers on it hopped into the room.

"Miss," squealed one of the girls, "Daisy's welly has come to life!"

The boot stopped.

"Don't be silly," said Miss Keane, who was busy rearranging her begonias. "Wellies don't move on their own."

The boot began to bounce on the spot.

The class giggled.

Miss Keane turned.

The boot stopped.

Miss Keane went back to her begonias.

The boot did a merry little tap dance.

The class screamed with laughter.

Miss Keane whirled round.

The boot didn't stop.

"How peculiar," said Miss Keane. She grabbed the boot.

"What have you got in here, Daisy?"

"Nothing, Miss," said Daisy. "I don't know anything about it." She gave Tom and Zack a hard stare.

"There must be *something* inside," said Miss Keane, tipping the boot upside down.

To the boys' horror, Toppo tumbled out onto the floor. The class immediately gathered round. The little Satnik took one look at them, put his paws over his ears and began to bounce up and down.

"Goodness me!" exclaimed Miss Keane. "What is that?"

"It's a rabbit," said Tom quickly.

"It doesn't look like a rabbit," said

Miss Keane. "It looks more like a very small zebra."

"Buzz!" said Toppo, hopefully.

"And it doesn't sound like a rabbit," added Miss Keane.

Daisy scooped Toppo up. "I'll tell you what sort of animal he is," she said.

Tom and Zack looked at each other in alarm. Had Daisy found out that Toppo wasn't from Earth at all?

"You won't know this one, Daisy," said Zack.

"Oh, yes, I will," said Daisy. To the boys' astonishment, she gave them a friendly wink. "This creature is a rare breed of rabbit," she announced loudly. "He's a zabbit."

"A zabbit?" repeated Miss Keane. "Are you sure?"

"Yes," said Daisy firmly. "Zabbits are rabbits with zebra stripes. My dad has taught me about every animal on Earth."

"Well, you must be right, then," said Miss Keane.

Tom's jaw dropped open. He couldn't believe it. Daisy had got them out of trouble.

"I think we'll keep this dear little creature as a pet," Miss Keane went on. "We'll be the only class to have a real live zabbit."

"Buzz!" Toppo nodded eagerly and his ears curled up in excitement.

"I think he likes that idea," said Miss Keane. "What shall we call him?"

"Toppo," said Tom and Zack together.

"A splendid name," laughed Miss Keane. "Do we all agree?"

The class cheered.

"That's settled, then," Miss Keane said brightly. "Now, go back to your spellings while I get everything ready for our new pet. Look after Toppo for me, Daisy."

"All right, Miss," said Daisy. "I'll give him a drink, but I'll need Tom and Zack to help."

While Miss Keane bashed about in the stock cupboard, Daisy took Toppo over to the sink. Tom and Zack followed. What was Daisy up to?

"I knew you were hiding something," said Daisy. "And I want to know the truth. Toppo is not an Earth animal. He's an alien, isn't he?"

"Well . . ." said Tom.

"Er . . ." said Zack.

"I promise not to tell anyone," added Daisy, smiling. She tickled Toppo under his chin. "He's really cute."

"I think we can trust her, boys," Toppo piped up.

Daisy nearly dropped him into the sink. "You can talk!" she gasped.

"Zoops!" said Toppo. "Of course I can."

"So can his friend, Fizz," Zack told her. "And there are others we haven't met yet."

"There are others?" asked Daisy in delight.

"Yes," said Tom. "They crash-landed in my pond."

"You mean *splash*-landed!" laughed Zack.

"Where are you from?" Daisy asked Toppo.

"I come from Saturn," said Toppo. "I'm a Satnik. I'm investigating Earth."

"It's cosmic," said Tom.

"Totally cosmic!" agreed Daisy.

"I'm going to enjoy living here," said Toppo, looking round the classroom. "I'll do lots of investigating, and tonight I'll make my nest in that nice drawer over there."

"Rabbits don't make nests," said Zack.

Miss Keane staggered out of the cupboard carrying a rabbit hutch.

"This is for Toppo," she said, putting it in the corner. "There is a good strong door so he can't escape and get lost."

"No!" cried Tom, Zack and Daisy together.

"Yes," said Miss Keane. "School pets must be put in cages. It's the rule."

She took Toppo from Daisy and put him inside. His little face peered through the wire.

"Buzz!" he said sadly.

"But he can't investigate if he's stuck in that hutch," Tom whispered to Zack and Daisy. "And he can't see his alien friends."

"Zabbits are free range, Miss Keane,"

called Daisy desperately. "You don't know what will happen if he's shut up."

"We can't have him wandering all over the classroom," said their teacher. "He'll get hurt." She clapped her hands. "Now, back to our lovely spellings. I hope you're ready for the test. *Fun, fun, fun for everyone!*"

"What are we going to do?" whispered Zack as they sat at their table again. "We need to rescue Toppo."

"I've got a plan," said Tom. "And it can't fail. I'll throw a blanket over Miss Keane's head and pretend it's an eclipse while you two smuggle the hutch out of the room."

"We haven't got a blanket," Zack pointed out.

"I hadn't thought of that," said Tom.

"Wait a minute . . . I've got a better plan! I'll sneak under her chair and shake it. You two shout, 'Earthquake!' and when everyone rushes out, you grab Toppo."

"I don't call that much of a plan," said Daisy. "Miss Keane is sure to see you crawling under her chair."

"Pens poised, everyone," called Miss Keane. "Here comes the first word . . . Goodness gracious!"

"That wasn't on the list, Miss," called someone.

But Miss Keane didn't answer. She was staring at the hutch. Everyone turned to look.

Creak!

All the nails were rising out of the wood.

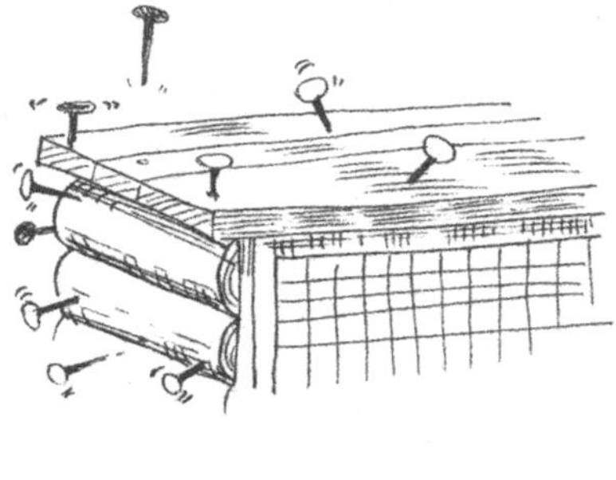

Ping!

They shot into the air.

Whee!

The roof flew off.

Crunch!

The walls fell flat.

Toppo stood in the wreckage, grinning at everyone.

"Well, I never!" gasped Miss Keane.

"I tried to tell you he's free range, Miss," said Daisy. "That always happens if you put a zabbit in a hutch. They don't like being shut in."

"I should have listened to you," said Miss Keane, mopping her brow. "But where will little Toppo sleep?"

"I think he'll find somewhere," said Tom.

"You'll have to leave a window open at night," put in Zack. "You don't want to come in tomorrow and find the school's collapsed!"

The bell rang.

Toppo hopped onto Tom's shoulder.

"What's that sound?" he said.

"That's the bell," explained Tom. "Now it's rung, we can go out to play."

Everyone rushed to the door. Miss Keane began to clear up the smashed bits of hutch. As they all piled into the playground, a Year Six monitor went by, clanging the bell.

"Interesting," said Toppo. "I'm going to investigate that."

"When it rings again we have to come back in for more lessons," added Daisy.

"Will I have to come back in, too?" asked Toppo.

"Yes," said Zack. "We all have to."

"Playtime's a lot better than lessons," said Tom, "but it's not long enough."

Toppo's eyes were full of mischief.

"And playtime doesn't end until the bell rings again?" he asked. "So if the bell happened to end up on the roof, would anyone be able to reach it?"

"Not without a ladder," said Tom.

"That's right," said Daisy with a grin.

"Zoops!" chuckled Toppo in delight. "Then it's time for another Top Toppo Trick!"

"Cosmic!" yelled Tom and Zack together.

REPORT

NAME

Toppo

EARTH IDENTITY

zabbit

REPORT

School is fun. It is also very strange.

Earthling children like tricks.

Earthling teachers make children do lots of work. They say it is fun.

Earthling children don't think it is fun.

They want to have more playtime and tricks.

I think I've fixed that.

LOOK OUT!

The *PETS FROM SPACE* are back.
If you don't like madness, **mayhem**
and mischief then
run away from this book!

But if you love jokes,
TRICKS and
fun then dive in!

Tom, Zack and Daisy meet a new **ALIEN** and
take the *PETS FROM SPACE* to the wildlife park.
What will happen when they meet elephants,
penguins and LIONS?
Will they be friends or will they be ***LUNCH***?